DISNEY · PIXAR

Beware of Dug!

Adapted by Annie Auerbach
Illustrated by Christian Robinson

A Random House PICTUREBACK® Book

Random House 🏠 New York

Copyright © 2009 Disney Enterprises, Inc./Pixar. All rights reserved. Published in the United States by Random House Children's Books, a division of Random House, Inc., 1745 Broadway, New York, NY 10019, and in Canada by Random House of Canada Limited, Toronto, in conjunction with Disney Enterprises, Inc. Pictureback, Random House, and the Random House colophon are registered trademarks of Random House, Inc.
Library of Congress Control Number: 2008939589
ISBN: 978-0-7364-2585-8
www.randomhouse.com/kids
Printed in the United States of America
10 9 8 7 6 5 4 3 2

Deep in a South American jungle, a dog named Dug was sniffing at the ground. He was on a mission to find a mysterious bird. Suddenly, he came upon an old man and a boy tugging a house!

The boy and the old man were surprised to meet Dug.
"Sit!" said the boy, whose name was Russell. Dug sat.
"Shake!" Russell said. Dug held out his paw.
"Speak!" Russell commanded.
"Hi there," said Dug. Russell and the old man, whose
name was Carl, were shocked. They had never heard
of a talking dog before.

"Hi THERE."

Dug showed Carl and Russell his high-tech collar. It allowed him to speak in any language.

SPEAKER

LIGHT

CAMERA

LANGUAGE DIAL

Suddenly, a giant bird leaped out of the bushes and tackled Dug.

"Hey! That is the bird!" Dug said excitedly. "May I take your bird as my prisoner?" he asked Carl.

"Be my guest," Carl said.

But the bird did not
want to be captured.
It followed Carl and
Russell. So Dug followed
them, too.

In another part of the jungle, three other dogs, named Alpha, Beta, and Gamma, were also hunting for the bird.

"Soon enough, the bird will be ours," Alpha told the other dogs.

"I wonder if Dug has found the bird on his *very special mission*," said Gamma, laughing. Dug couldn't do anything right, so Alpha had sent him out alone.

"Come in, Dug," Alpha said, using Beta's collar to contact Dug. "Have you seen the bird?"

"Why, yes," replied Dug. "I am here with the bird."

"Impossible!" exclaimed Alpha when he saw the bird on the video screen. Barking fiercely, the three dogs set out to find Dug—and the bird.

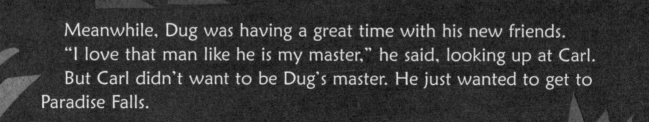

Meanwhile, Dug was having a great time with his new friends.
"I love that man like he is my master," he said, looking up at Carl.
But Carl didn't want to be Dug's master. He just wanted to get to
Paradise Falls.

"I am nobody's master, get it?" he said to Dug.

But Dug wasn't listening. He was more interested in playing fetch with the tennis balls on Carl's cane.

Dug stayed with his new friends that night. He planned to take the bird to his pack the next day.

But he didn't get the chance. The next morning, the bird left!

Just then, Alpha, Gamma, and Beta burst out of the bushes. They surrounded Dug, Carl, and Russell.

"Where's the bird?" Alpha asked Dug. "You said you had the bird."

Dug had to tell Alpha that the bird had escaped.

"You lost it!" Alpha snarled. "Why do I not have a surprised feeling?"

Alpha decided to take Carl and
Russell to his master, Charles Muntz.
Muntz had spent many years living
in a cave. Pleased to have visitors,
he invited Carl and Russell inside.

Meanwhile, the dog pack was deciding what to do with Dug.
"He has lost the bird," said Alpha. "Put him in the Cone of Shame."

"I do not like the Cone of Shame,"
Dug said, hanging his head sadly.

Then the dogs returned to their master. Muntz had asked Carl and Russell to dinner. The dogs served the guests food while Muntz told them why he was there. He'd spent a lifetime searching for the "Monster of Paradise Falls." As Muntz described the creature, Carl realized that he was after the bird!

Just then, Carl spotted the bird—standing on the roof of his floating house!

Muntz saw the bird, too. He thought Carl was trying to steal it from him.

"Get them!" he ordered his dogs.

Carl, Russell, and the bird ran for their lives.
The dogs chased after them, barking angrily.
"Get back!" Carl shouted at the dogs.
But there was no stopping the pack.

Suddenly, an avalanche of boulders tumbled down in front of Alpha and the dog pack, blocking their path.

"Go on, Master!" someone shouted. "I will stop the dogs!"

It was Dug! He had caused the avalanche to save Carl and Russell.

Dug knew that his old master would be angry—but he didn't care. He had new friends, and their adventures were just beginning! Best of all, now those other dogs knew to *beware of Dug!*